# BENJAMIN BUNNY

Based on the original story by
Beatrix Potter
with all new illustrations

Cover illustration by
Anita Nelson
Book illustrations by
Sam Thiewes

**Publications International, Ltd.**

One morning, Benjamin Bunny sat in the sun by the side of the road. He pricked his ears to the trit-trot, trit-trot of a pony and cart. Mr. McGregor was driving the pony cart, and beside him sat Mrs. McGregor, wearing her best bonnet.

As soon as they had passed, Benjamin Bunny got an idea. With a hop, skip, and a jump he set off to visit his cousins who lived in the woods behind Mr. McGregor's garden.

Benjamin's aunt, Old Mrs. Rabbit, made her living by knitting mittens and scarves. But Benjamin had not come to visit his aunt. He was looking for his cousin Peter. He went around the back of the fir tree and nearly stumbled over Peter. Peter was sitting by himself, and he didn't look too happy. He was dressed only in a red cotton handkerchief, which he held tightly around him.

"Peter," whispered Benjamin, "where are your clothes?"

Peter told Benjamin how he had lost his shoes and coat. Mr. McGregor was using them as a scarecrow. Benjamin said he had seen Mrs. McGregor wearing her best bonnet so the McGregors would probably be gone all day. He and Peter could go to Mr. McGregor's garden and rescue Peter's clothes.

Peter and Benjamin climbed Mr. McGregor's garden wall and saw Peter's coat and shoes hanging like a scarecrow. A knitted cap topped off the scarecrow's outfit.

Benjamin said, "We will get dirty if we squeeze under the gate. We should climb down the pear tree."

Peter fell into the garden head first. But he landed in a soft lettuce bed. They took Peter's clothes off the scarecrow poles. It had rained, and his shoes were full of water. His coat had shrunk, and all the buttons were missing. Benjamin tried on the cap, but it was too big for him. Now that Peter had his clothes, they could use the handkerchief for something else.

Benjamin began to fill the red handkerchief with onions, as a present for Peter's mother. He felt perfectly at home here and ate a lettuce leaf. Benjamin said he often came to Mr. McGregor's garden with his father to get lettuce for their dinner. Mr. McGregor's lettuce was certainly very tasty.

Peter did not eat anything, though. He was not enjoying himself. He kept hearing noises. He wanted to go home.

The little bunnies knew they would not be able to climb up the pear tree with their bundle of onions. So they walked to the other end of the garden, among the flowerpots, baskets, and tools. Peter heard more noises than ever! Suddenly, his eyes were as big as lollipops!

Benjamin took one look, then he and Peter hid themselves—and the onions—under a large basket. They had seen a big barn cat napping in the afternoon sun!

The cat awoke and stretched. She walked to the upside-down basket and gave it a sniff. She sat right down on top of the basket! (She must have liked the smell of onions!) And there she sat—for five hours.

The sun was setting over the trees in the woods, but still the cat sat on the basket. Peter and Benjamin were trapped. It was quite dark, and the smell of onions was awful. Peter Rabbit and Benjamin Bunny began to cry.

Through their tears, the two bunnies heard a pitter patter of stones falling from the garden wall. The cat looked up and saw Old Mr. Benjamin Bunny walking along the top of the wall, looking for his son.

Old Mr. Bunny was not afraid of cats at all. He jumped from the wall onto the cat and pushed her off the basket! Then he kicked her into the greenhouse, scratching off a bit of fur. The cat was too surprised to scratch back!

After Mr. Bunny had locked the greenhouse door, he came back to the basket and pulled Benjamin and Peter out by the ears. He scolded the two bad rabbits all the way home!

When Mr. McGregor returned, he was puzzled over the scarecrow and about the cat locked in the greenhouse. And as for old Mrs. Rabbit, she was so glad to see Peter she quite forgot to scold him for wandering off.